SAVED FROM SCRAP

by

The Rev. W. Awdry

with illustrations by
C. Reginald Dalby

Grolier

Cows!

EDWARD the blue engine was getting old. His bearings were worn, and he clanked as he puffed along. He was taking twenty empty cattle trucks to a market-town.

The sun shone, the birds sang, and some cows grazed in a field by the line.

"Come on! come on! come on!" puffed Edward.

"Oh! oh! oh! oh!" screamed the trucks.

Edward puffed and clanked; the trucks rattled and screamed. The cows were not used to trains; the noise and smoke disturbed them.

They twitched up their tails and ran.

They galloped across the field, broke through the fence, and charged the train between the thirteenth and fourteenth trucks. The coupling broke, and the last seven trucks left the rails. They were not damaged, and stayed upright. They ran for a short way along the sleepers before stopping.

Edward felt a jerk but didn't take much notice.

He was used to trucks.

"Bother those trucks!" he thought. "Why can't they come quietly?" He ran on to the next station before either he or his Driver realised what had happened.

When Gordon and Henry heard about the accident, they laughed and laughed. "Fancy allowing cows to break his train! They wouldn't dare do that to US. WE'd show them!" they boasted.

Edward pretended not to mind, but Toby was cross.

"You couldn't help it, Edward," he said. "They've never met cows. I have, and I know the trouble they are."

Some days later Gordon rushed through Edward's station.

"Poop poop!" he whistled, "mind the cows!"

"Haha, haha, haha!" he chortled, panting up the hill.

"Hurry, hurry, hurry!" puffed Gordon.

"Don't make such a fuss! Don't make such a fuss!" grumbled his coaches. They rumbled over the viaduct and roared through the next station.

A long straight stretch of line lay ahead. In the distance was a bridge. It had high parapets each side.

It seemed to Gordon that there was something on the bridge. His Driver thought so too. "Whoa, Gordon!" he said, and shut off steam.

"Pooh!" said Gordon, "it's only a cow!"

"SHOOH! SHOOH!" he hissed, moving slowly on to the bridge.

But the cow wouldn't "Shooh"! She had lost her calf, and felt lonely "Mooooh!" she said sadly, walking towards him.

Gordon stopped!

His Driver, Fireman and some Passengers tried to send her away, but she wouldn't go, so they gave it up.

Presently Henry arrived with a train from the other direction.

"What's this?" he said grandly. "A cow? I'll soon settle *her*. Be off! be off!" he hissed; but the cow turned and "moohed" at him. Henry backed away. "I don't want to hurt her," he said.

Drivers, Firemen and Passengers again tried to move the cow, but failed. Henry's Guard went back and put detonators on the line to protect his train. At the nearest station he told them about the cow.

"That must be Bluebell," said a Porter thoughtfully, "her calf is here, ready to go to market. We'll take it along."

So they unloaded the calf and took it to the bridge.

"Mooh! mooh!" wailed the calf. "Mooh Mooh!" bellowed Bluebell.

She nuzzled her calf happily, and the Porter led them away.

The two trains started.

"Not a word."

"Keep it dark," whispered Gordon and Henry as they passed; but the story soon spread.

"Well, well, well!" chuckled Edward, "two big engines afraid of one cow!"

"Afraid——Rubbish," said Gordon huffily. "We didn't want the poor thing to hurt herself by running against us. We stopped so as not to excite her. You see what I mean, my dear Edward."

"Yes, Gordon," said Edward gravely.

Gordon felt somehow that Edward "saw" only too well.

Saved from Scrap

THERE is a scrap-yard near Edward's station. It is full of rusty old cars and machinery. They are brought there to be broken up. The pieces are loaded into trucks, and Edward pulls them to the Steelworks, where they are melted down and used again.

One day Edward saw a Traction-engine in the Yard.

"Hullo!" he said, "you're not broken and rusty. What are you doing there?"

"I'm Trevor," said the Traction-engine sadly, "they are going to break me up next week."

"What a shame!" said Edward.

"My Driver says I only need some paint, Brasso, and oil, to be as good as new," Trevor went on sadly, "but it's no good, my Master doesn't want me. I suppose it's because I'm old-fashioned."

Edward snorted indignantly, "People say *I'm* old fashioned, but I don't care. The Fat Controller says I'm a Useful Engine."

"My Driver says I'm useful too," replied Trevor. "I sometimes feel ill, but I don't give up like these Tractors; I struggle on and finish the job. I've never broken down in my life," he ended proudly.

"What work did you do?" asked Edward kindly.

"My Master would send us from farm to farm. We threshed the corn, hauled logs, sawed timber, and did lots of other work. We made friends at all the farms, and saw them every year. The children loved to see us come. They followed us in crowds, and watched us all day long. My Driver would sometimes give them rides."

Trevor shut his eyes——remembering——

"I like children," he said simply. "Oh yes, I like children."

"Broken up, what a shame! Broken up, what a shame!" clanked Edward as he went back to work. "I *must* help Trevor, I *must*!"

He thought of the people he knew, who liked engines. Edward had lots of friends, but strangely none of them had room for a Traction-engine at home!

"It's a shame! It's a shame!" he hissed as he brought his coaches to the station.

Then——

"Peep! peep!" he whistled, "why didn't I think of him before?"

Waiting there on the platform was the very person.

" 'Morning Charlie, 'Morning Sid. Hullo Edward, you look upset!

"What's the matter, Charlie?" he asked the Driver.

"There's a Traction-engine in the scrap-yard, Vicar; he'll be broken up next week, and it's a shame. Jem Cole says he never drove a better engine."

"Do save him, Sir! You've got room, Sir!"

"Yes, Edward, I've got room," laughed the Vicar, "but I don't need a Traction-engine!"

"He'll saw wood, and give children rides. Do buy him, Sir, please!"

"We'll see," said the Vicar, and climbed into the train.

Jem Cole came on Saturday afternoon. "The Reverend's coming to see you, Trevor; maybe he'll buy you."

"Do you think he will?" asked Trevor hopefully.

"He will when I've lit your fire, and cleaned you up," said Jem.

When the Vicar and his two boys arrived in the evening, Trevor was blowing off steam. He hadn't felt so happy for months.

"Watch this, Reverence," called Jem, and Trevor chuffered happily about the Yard.

"Oh Daddy, DO buy him," pleaded the boys, jumping up and down in their excitement.

"Now *I'll* try," and the Vicar climbed up beside Jem.

"Show your paces, Trevor," he said, and drove him about the Yard.

Then he went into the office, and came out smiling. "I've got him cheap, Jem, cheap."

"D'ye hear that, Trevor?" cried Jem. "The Reverend's saved you, and you'll live at the Vicarage now."

"Peep! Peep!" whistled Trevor happily.

"Will you drive him home for me, Jem, and take these scallywags with you? They won't want to come in the car when there's a Traction-engine to ride on!"

Trevor's home in the Vicarage Orchard is close to the railway, and he sees Edward every day. His paint is spotless and his brass shines like gold.

He saws firewood in winter, and Jem sometimes borrows him when a tractor fails. Trevor likes doing his old jobs, but his happiest day is the Church Fête. Then, with a long wooden seat bolted to his bunker, he chuffers round the Orchard giving rides to children.

Long afterwards you will see him shut his eyes——remembering——

"I like children," he whispers happily.